This Book Belongs to:

. . . .

First published in Great Britain in 1999 by Andersen Press Ltd., 20 Vauxhall Bridge Road, London SW1V 2SA.
This paperback edition first published in 2008 by Andersen Press Ltd.
Published in Australia by Random House Australia Pty., Level 3, 100 Pacific Highway, North Sydney, NSW 2060.
Text copyright © Jeanne Willis, 1999. Illustration copyright © Tony Ross, 1999.
The rights of Jeanne Willis and Tony Ross to be identified as the author and illustrator
of this work have been asserted by them in accordance with the Copyright, Designs and Patents Act, 1988.
All rights reserved. Colour separated in Switzerland by Photolitho AG, Zürich.
Printed and bound in Singapore by Tien Wah Press.

10   9   8   7   6   5   4   3   2   1

British Library Cataloguing in Publication Data available.

ISBN 978 1 84270 752 4

This book has been printed on acid-free paper

The Boy Who Lost His Bellybutton

written by Jeanne Willis
and illustrated by Tony Ross

ANDERSEN PRESS

Once there was a little boy who lost his bellybutton.

It was there when he went to sleep
but when he woke up it was gone.
So he went into the jungle to look for it.

On the way, he met a giraffe.

"I've lost my bellybutton,"
explained the boy. "Do you know
where it is?"
"Search me!" said the giraffe.
So the boy fetched a ladder
and searched the giraffe.
He found a button, but it wasn't his.

"It's mine," said the giraffe.
"I've had it since the day I was born."

So the boy asked the gorilla.
"Have you found a bellybutton anywhere?"
"Yes," said the gorilla. "Right here."
And it stuck out its tummy.

"Very nice," said the boy, "but it's not mine."
"My mother gave it to me," said the gorilla.

Just then, the boy spotted a lion
sleeping on its back in the long grass.
He crept up and went through its fur
with a long tooth comb.
The lion opened one eye.
"I was wondering if you'd borrowed
my bellybutton," said the boy politely.

"Why would I? I've got a perfectly good
one of my own," said the lion. "See?"

The boy saw.
"Have all animals got bellybuttons?" he asked.
"Hands up everyone who's got a bellybutton!"
roared the lion.

"Look, I've got a huge one," bellowed the elephant.

"I've got a weeny one," squeaked the mouse.

"I've got a warty one," grunted the warthog.

"I've got a stripey one," snorted the zebra.

"And I've got a muddy one," gurgled the hippopotamus.

But the crocodile lay in the swamp as if it had
something to hide.
"How about crocodiles? Do they have bellybuttons?"
"They might do," sneered the crocodile.
"Show me!" cried the boy.
So the crocodile rolled over . . .

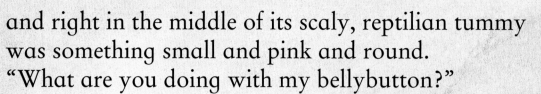

and right in the middle of its scaly, reptilian tummy
was something small and pink and round.
"What are you doing with my bellybutton?"
shouted the little boy.
"I'm washing the fluff out for you," said the crocodile.
"Thanks," said the boy. "Can I have it back now?"
"Certainly," smiled the crocodile. "Come and get it."

So the boy took off his clothes . . .

He waded right into the swamp.
And . . .

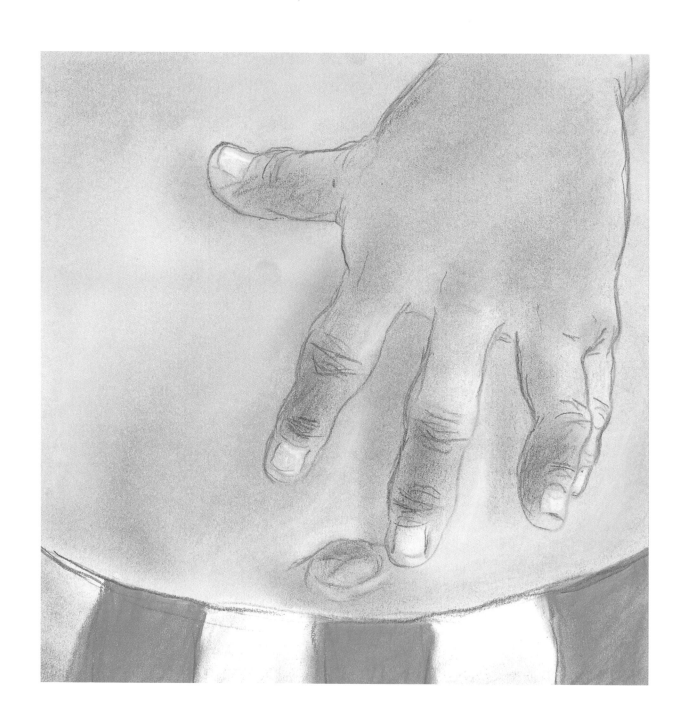

he GRABBED it!

Other books by Jeanne Willis and Tony Ross:

9781842705261

MISERY MOO

Jeanne Willis   Tony Ross

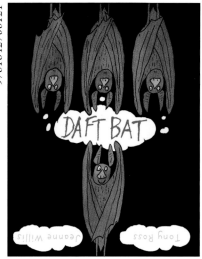

9781842706121

DAFT BAT

Jeanne Willis   Tony Ross

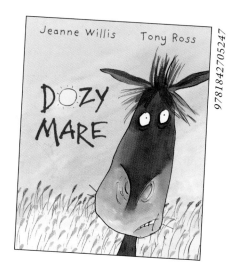

9781842705247

Jeanne Willis   Tony Ross

DOZY MARE

9781842705711

The Really RUDE Rhino

Jeanne Willis   Tony Ross

9781842705667

Jeanne Willis   Tony Ross

Shhh!

'Delightful and wise' GUARDIAN

9781842705391

COTTONWOOL COLIN

Jeanne Willis and Tony Ross

9781842704264

Tadpole's Promise

Jeanne Willis

Tony Ross

9781842703427

Grill Pan Eddy

Jeanne Willis and Tony Ross